Kittens

Julie Murray

Abdo
BABY ANIMALS
Kids

abdopublishing.com

Published by Abdo Kids, a division of ABDO, PO Box 398166, Minneapolis, Minnesota 55439.

Printed in the United States of America, North Mankato, Minnesota.

052017

092017

THIS BOOK CONTAINS RECYCLED MATERIALS

Photo Credits: iStock, Shutterstock

Production Contributors: Teddy Borth, Jennie Forsberg, Grace Hansen

Design Contributors: Christina Doffing, Candice Keimig, Dorothy Toth

Publisher's Cataloging in Publication Data

Names: Murray, Julie, 1969-, author.

Title: Kittens / by Julie Murray.

Description: Minneapolis, Minnesota : Abdo Kids, 2018 | Series: Baby animals | Includes bibliographical references and index.

Identifiers: LCCN 2016962293 | ISBN 9781532100031 (lib. bdg.) | ISBN 9781532100727 (ebook) | ISBN 9781532101274 (Read-to-me ebook)

Subjects: LCSH: Kittens--Juvenile literature. | Kittens--Infancy--Juvenile literature.

Classification: DDC 636.8--dc23

LC record available at http://lccn.loc.gov/2016962293

Table of Contents

Kittens

A baby cat is a kitten.

A **litter** often has 1 to 9 kittens.

Kittens cannot see or hear at birth.

Mothers keep them safe.

Kittens sleep and eat. They drink their mother's milk.

They play together.

They have soft **fur**. They come in many colors.

They can be **adopted** at 12 weeks old.

Jake likes his kitten's

white paws!

Watch a Tabby Kitten Grow!

newborn

6 weeks

12 weeks

1 year

Glossary

adopt
to become the owner and caretaker of a pet.

litter
a number of young produced at one birth by a mammal.

fur
the very fine hair of some animals.

Index

abdokids.com

Use this code to log on to abdokids.com and access crafts, games, videos, and more!